Ian Beck's
LOST
in the
SNOW

Hippo

For Lily

Teddy Bears have such a quiet life,
don't they?

Scholastic Children's Books
Commonwealth House, 1-19 New Oxford Street
London WC1A 1NU, UK
a division of Scholastic Ltd
London ~ New York ~ Toronto ~ Sydney ~ Auckland
Mexico City~New Delhi~Hong Kong

First published in hardback in the UK by Scholastic Ltd, 1998
First published in paperback in the UK by Scholastic Ltd, 1998
This paperback bind-up edition first published in the UK by Scholastic Ltd, 2004

Copyright © Ian Beck, 1998

ISBN 0 439 96343 5

After a night of snow, the world was white.
Lily and Teddy looked through the window.
"We must go out and play."

"Wrap up nice and warm," said Mum. "But we'd better leave Teddy here, we don't want him to get lost."

"Poor Teddy." Lily wrapped him in a scarf, and put him on the window ledge, so that he could see the snow. "Be careful now," she said.

Before they went out, Mum banged shut the window. She didn't see Teddy sitting out there.

Whoosh! Teddy was catapulted high into the cold air.

Bump! He slid down a roof!
Boing! He bounced off an icy washing line . . .

. . . and flew on, far above the houses and trees.

Until he landed . . . plomp! . . . head first in a snow drift.

He pulled himself up out of the snow.

Teddy took a deep breath in the wonderful
crisp air. He began to explore but his paws
slipped on a plank of wood.

He lost his balance and whoops! He was sliding
fast down the steep hill!

He was snowboarding. It was such
fun that he tried it over and over again.

Until he ended upside down against a tree in a field of fresh snow.

He stomped round and round, up and down,
making lots of deep crunchy pawprints.

Then he decided to make a big snow bear and,
when he had finished, he gave it his own warm
scarf to wear.

He spotted an icy puddle that looked just right for sliding on. He ran at top speed and . . .

Wheeeee . . . eee . . . eee. . . ee . . .

. . . he slid right across.

And fell flat on his face in the cold snow.

When he stood up, his paws were cold. He felt lost and alone. It started to snow again.

The frosty wind blew up and it snowed harder
and harder. Teddy began to trudge home.

But he was soon lost in the snow.

After what seemed a very long time,
he heard a kindly voice. "Hop on here and
I'll take you home."

Teddy snuggled up under a warm blanket in a whizzing sleigh.

Soon Teddy was dropped safely home, back on to the window ledge. "I must go," called the voice. "I have much to do . . ."

Lily brought Teddy in from the cold.
"Come on," she said, "let's get you warm."

"You missed all the fun today, Teddy," said Lily,
"but now it is time for bed."

Lily hugged Teddy. "Tonight is a special night," she whispered.

Good Night, Lily. Kiss kiss.
And Good Night, Teddy. Sleep tight.
But we know what really happened, don't we?

Good Night, Lily. Kiss kiss.
And Good Night, Teddy. Sleep tight.
But we know what really happened, don't we?

When Lily and Mum came back, Lily said,
"What a good Bear! You missed all the fun.
Never mind. Come on, time to go home."

. . . he landed, very gently, with the softest
bump, just where he had started.

But after one big heave, the wind lifted him,
above the trees, over the hills, and far away,
all the way back, until . . .

And so they did. It took a little while to get Teddy into the air, after all the jelly and honey buns.

When Teddy woke up, it was getting late.
"How will I get back?" he said.
"Don't worry," said the bears, "we'll help."

. . . Teddy Bears' picnic."
They feasted on jelly and honey buns and
lemonade, and then they all had a little sleep.

"You landed in our best jelly," they said.
"Never mind, don't be shy, tuck in, it's a
party, it's a . . ."

Then slowly, out of the shadows they stepped,
first one, then two, three, four, and then more,
and more, and more, Teddy Bears.

When he looked up Teddy saw bright
eyes looking at him. He felt frightened.
Teddy was alone in the woods.

. . . he landed 'plop', into something green and sticky! He heard voices whispering in the bushes.

And Teddy fell with it, faster and faster, lower and lower, down, down into the woods until . . .

Then suddenly the wind dropped, and the kite began to fall down through the clouds.

Higher, higher and higher still, but this was fun!

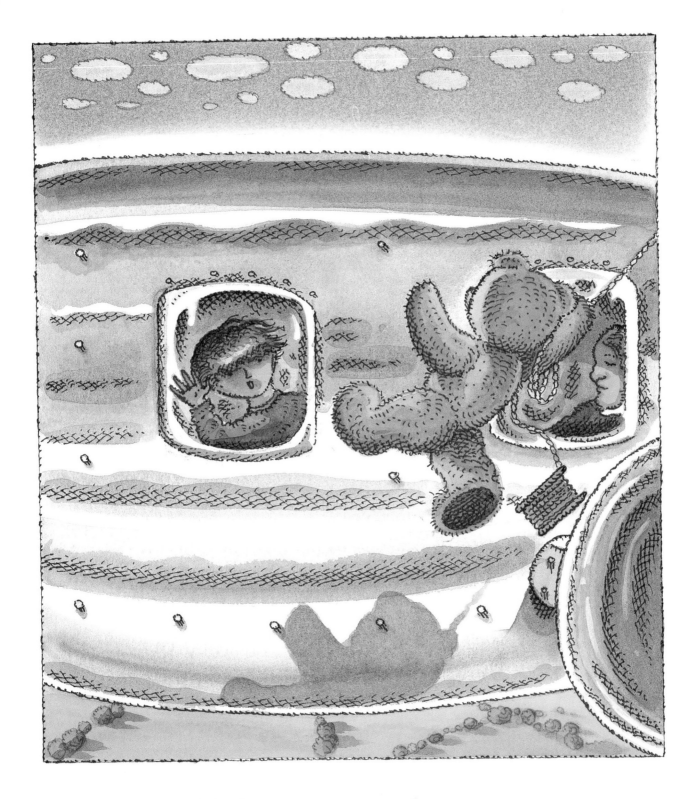

He flew as high as an aeroplane.
"Whee!" waved Teddy.

. . . flying! High up in the air. Now he was
higher than the clouds.

He held on to the kite string with all his might because he was . . .

As the kite lifted higher and higher, Teddy was
dragged through a hedge backwards.

Teddy bump, bump, bumped along the ground.

He was lifted over some prickly brambles and just missed a cowpat.

Suddenly a great gust of wind blew, and
tugged at the red kite. The kite lifted,
and, oh dear, tugged at Teddy.

So Mum and Lily set off, leaving Teddy all alone to guard the picnic.

After the picnic Mum said, "Let's fly
a kite. Which one shall we take?"
Lily chose the yellow one.

"Poor old Teddy," said Lily. "There's none for you, but you don't need a picnic, do you?"

They laid out the cloth for the picnic.
Lily set Teddy down under a tree.

They chose the perfect spot.

At last they reached the top of Windy Hill.

Halfway up the steep hill, Lily asked, "Are we nearly there yet?"

"Not far," said Mum. "We'll be there soon."

Lily asked if Teddy could come and, of course,
he could. So they gathered up the picnic things
and the kites, and set off.

It was a perfect Spring day. "Come on," said Lily. "I want to go on a picnic and fly my kite. Let's ask Mum."

For Lily

Teddy Bears have such a quiet life,
don't they?

Scholastic Children's Books
Commonwealth House, 1-19 New Oxford Street
London WC1A 1NU, UK
a division of Scholastic Ltd
London ~ New York ~ Toronto ~ Sydney ~ Auckland
Mexico City ~ New Delhi ~ Hong Kong

First published in hardback in the UK by Scholastic Ltd, 2000
First published in paperback in the UK by Scholastic Ltd, 2000
This paperback bind-up edition first published in the UK by Scholastic Ltd, 2004

Copyright © Ian Beck, 2000

ISBN 0 439 96343 5

Ian Beck's
ALONE
in the
WOODS

Hippo